For This Land

Meg's Prairie Diary

· Book Two ·

by Kate McMullan

Scholastic Inc. New York

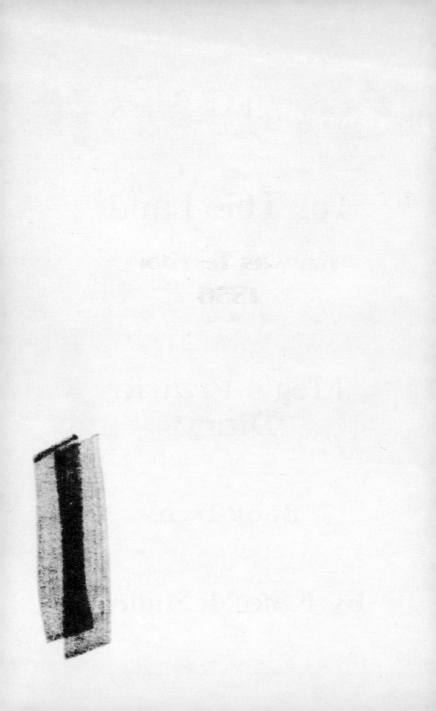

Kansas Territory
1856

July 8, 1856

It is Christmas in July! Mother brought me a new diary from St. Louis. She planned to save it for Christmas. But I had finished my first diary. So she gave it to me today.

What a different life I would be writing about if Mother had not caught cholera last spring. Then she never would have had Father put my brother, Pres, and me on a riverboat. We would never have gone up the Missouri River in the care of their friend, Dr. Baer. We would not be living in a small cabin with Mother's sister, my Aunt Margaret, and Uncle Aubert, and my cousins, George, Charlie, and John. Mother and my little sister, Grace, would not

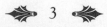 3

be here, either. And Father would not be on his way to Kansas Territory, also known as K.T. But Mother *did* catch cholera. And here we are.

Aunt Margaret is singing with happiness to have Mother and Grace here. Once she was the only woman in the cabin. Now there are four. Aunt Margaret says it is a terrible shame that women cannot vote in elections. But in our cabin, when anything must be decided, we women will have a vote.

Later

I helped Mother unpack. She will sleep in my cozy quilt room now. She grew teary getting out the photographs of my brothers, Lee and Larry. She said it was the hardest thing she has ever done, leaving her babies behind in the St. Louis cemetery.

I will sleep up in the loft now. Grace will,

too. Aunt Margaret hung a blue-and-white quilt from the rafters. George, Charlie, John, and Pres sleep on the white side of the quilt. Grace and I call our side the Blue Quilt Room.

Later

Uncle Aubert and George have finished building the summer kitchen. It is next to the cabin. They made it with sod bricks dug from the earth. They moved the cookstove into it. Now our cabin will not be heated up when we cook.

If only Father were here! Mother says we can start watching for him in two weeks.

July 9, 1850

It was hot in the loft last night. The boys pulled themselves out the window and climbed

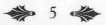

onto the roof to cool off. I wanted to go, too. But I was afraid Grace would try to follow me. So I only stuck my head out the window.

When I looked out my window in St. Louis, I saw big, brick houses. And fancy carriages passing by. Now when I look out I see the shapes of three big, flat-topped hills against the sky. George says one is Bald Mound. One is Blue Mound. The biggest is Mount Oread. There are no trees on the top of these mounds. George says the Shawnees used to burn them off each year. That way their scouts could stand on top of a mound and see for miles.

Back in St. Louis, our maid, Nellie, woke me in the morning. Now I wake up with the sun. This morning, Charlie, John, and Pres ran out to the prairie to collect cow chips. George, Grace, and I went to the barn. I fed Mollie the cow, her calves, and Kip the ox. George fed the horses, Bay and Star. Grace fed the chickens.

Once the animals were fed, Uncle Aubert set an empty barrel on the wagon bed. He hitched Kip to the wagon. Grace and I led him down to the stream. Our gray cat, Mouser, came, too. I filled buckets in the stream and poured water into the barrel. Grace splashed in the stream. She is only four and needs to play. But it was hard to work and keep an eye on her. At last, I made up a bucket-counting game, and got that barrel filled. We led Kip up the hill, hungry for a breakfast of Aunt Margaret's johnnycakes.

In St. Louis, Mrs. Potter cooked for us. But Mother says surely she can make johnnycakes.

Later

My friend Lily Vanbeek rode to our cabin this evening on her very own pony. She calls him Honey. Lily let me ride him. My first

pony ride! Uncle Aubert says a pony is a fine way for a young lady to get around on the prairie.

Lily told me a wonderful secret. Come spring, her mother will have another baby! Lily has six brothers. She asked me to pray for a baby girl.

Later

Tonight after supper we all sat on the cabin steps to catch the breeze. We saw a wagon coming. Uncle Aubert went quietly into the cabin to get his rifle. Pres asked why. Uncle Aubert only said, "Let's see who it is." I believe he thought it might be a Border Ruffian.

Ruffians come over the border to K.T. from Missouri or other states that allow slavery. Uncle Aubert says they are troublemakers. But

it was no Ruffian coming to our cabin. It was Mr. Jasper Young, the traveling photographer.

Aunt Margaret fixed Mr. Young a plate of supper. As he ate, he told us news he has heard in his travels. He said we have a new governor who believes slavery should be allowed in K.T. Uncle Aubert said this is terrible news.

Charlie and John brought a big pile of hay into the cabin. They put quilts on it to make Mr. Young a "prairie feather bed." When it grew dark, everyone turned in. Everyone except Uncle Aubert. He sat on the steps, brooding.

I sat down beside him. I asked him what was wrong. Uncle Aubert told me he is worried about K.T. He said in the last election here, a judge declared that if a man had been in K.T. for one hour, he could vote. Thousands of Border Ruffians came to K.T. They voted for

candidates who favored slavery. These men won. Now K.T. has a pro-slavery government. Uncle Aubert says it is a bogus government, not fairly elected. And now they have made it a crime even to speak out against slavery.

Uncle Aubert says K.T. will have another election soon. Men will vote on how Kansas should enter the United States. Will it be a slave state? Or will it be a free state where slavery is not allowed? It is all up to the election. Uncle Aubert says that if Kansas becomes a slave state, it will tip the balance in favor of slavery all over the country. Then, he said, it is likely that slavery will never end.

The Ruffians are part of a pro-slavery army. Its soldiers are trying to drive Free-State men out of K.T. so they cannot vote in the election. But men who are against slavery have formed an army, too. It is called the Free-State Militia.

Uncle Aubert says these armies are fighting for the future of Kansas.

Uncle Aubert took to brooding again. So I came up to bed. Now I am worried about K.T., too. Why did I have to ask Uncle Aubert what was wrong?

July 12, 1856

This morning, Mr. Young showed us some photographs he took in Lawrence last spring. The first was of a man named John Brown. His eyes looked fierce, and I said so. Mr. Young smiled. He seemed glad to have captured this quality in John Brown. He said John Brown is a fierce fighter against slavery in our land.

Another photograph showed the Free State Hotel. Still another showed a newspaper office. Mr. Young said it was *The Herald of Freedom*.

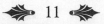

Pres said, "Harold who?" Mr. Young said that a "herald" is a messenger bringing important news. And Pres said, "Like, 'Hark! The herald angels sing?'" Mr. Young said, "Exactly." He said *The Herald of Freedom* was a messenger for freedom in K.T.

Then Mr. Young held up a photograph he took in Lawrence last week. It showed ruins of buildings that had burned to the ground. One was the Free State Hotel. The other was *The Herald of Freedom*.

Mr. Young said the Ruffians burned them down. They destroyed *The Herald of Freedom* printing press. They threw thousands of lead letters used for setting type into the river. For Ruffians do not believe in freedom for everyone, Mr. Young said. Especially not for Negro slaves.

All this happened in May. Mother sent Pres and me to K.T. in May so we would not catch

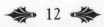

cholera. Mother said she never would have sent us had she known what was going on in Kansas.

Bedtime

I will blow out my candle now. I will pray for a sister for Lily.

July 13, 1856

Grace and I led Kip up from the stream this morning. When we reached the top of the hill, we saw smoke pouring from the summer kitchen. We feared it was going up in flames! But it was only Mother, making johnnycakes.

We ate hard biscuits for breakfast.

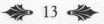

July 15, 1856

Uncle Aubert is taking some chickens into Lawrence this afternoon. The grasshoppers ate all his corn. So he will trade the chickens for cornmeal. He says Mother and I may go with him!

Bedtime

I saw so much in Lawrence today!

I saw three huge round holes dug in the ground. They are called "mud forts." They are nearly as deep as a man is tall. Uncle Aubert says if Ruffians attack, Free-State soldiers with rifles will go down into the mud forts to defend the town. They can pop up from the forts and shoot at Ruffians. Then they can duck down to keep from being shot.

I hope they never have to do this!

 14

Our first stop was the Dry Goods Shop. Uncle Aubert took in the crate of chickens. He got six sacks of cornmeal in return. A thermometer outside the store read 105 degrees. And it was in the shade!

On our way to the bank, we passed by the rubble where *The Herald of Freedom* and the Free State Hotel once stood. It was a sad sight.

We also passed the Emigrant Aid Society office. Part of the office is used for the Lawrence School. I asked Uncle Aubert when it will start. And he said, "When the Ruffians go home." Go home now, Ruffians!

At the bank, Uncle Aubert traded his gold dollars for the new paper banknotes. The President wants everyone to use them now. Aunt Margaret does not like paper money. But Uncle Aubert says he trusts it because every dollar is backed up by gold kept in Washington.

Our last stop was the post office. There was

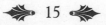

no letter from Father. But there was a package from the Emigrant Aid Society in Boston. Uncle Aubert says this society is strongly against slavery. They want Kansas to become a Free State. So they send what they can to support the Free-State settlers in Kansas.

The whole way home, I wondered what might be inside that package. But when Aunt Margaret opened it, there were only old boys' shoes. Aunt Margaret was glad. She says shoes are hard to come by in K.T. But George, Charlie, and John are always barefoot. Pres is, too. It is a pity there were no girls' shoes in the package.

July 17, 1856

I have a pony!

This morning, Uncle Aubert asked me to come out to the barn. And there stood a sweet brown pony, eating hay. "She is yours, Meg,"

he said. The pony's name is Sally. Uncle Aubert bought her from a neighbor who is now too old to ride. He says when it cools off, I can ride Sally over to show Lily.

Sally has big brown eyes. She has a big belly, too. I am so happy she is mine!

July 18, 1856

I no longer have a pony.

Yesterday afternoon, Uncle Aubert boosted me up onto Sally's back. Sally began trotting down the path. At the lightning-struck oak, I pulled the reins to turn Sally right, toward the Vanbeek's cabin. But Sally did not turn. I pulled the reins with all my might. But Sally kept trotting straight for Blue Mound. There was nothing to do but sit on her back and be bounced.

At last, we came to a cabin at the foot of

Blue Mound. Now I knew I had bounced for three miles, for our cabin is that far from Blue Mound. Sally trotted past the cabin and straight to the barn behind it. She began eating hay. I slipped off her back.

I walked toward the cabin. My heart was pounding. Was it a Ruffian's cabin? I called, "Anyone home?"

A voice answered. "Come in!"

The cabin was dark inside. But I made out an old person sitting in a rocker. She said she was Mrs. Biggs. She was small. Her silver hair was knotted on top of her head. Mrs. Biggs asked if I had a kind heart. I said I hoped I did. She asked if I could write. I said yes. She asked many questions. But she never asked why I had come to her cabin.

At last, Mrs. Biggs told me that she would soon be going to her heavenly reward. She said that as long as I was there, I might as well take

 18

down her last wishes. She told me where to find ink, pen, and paper. Then Mrs. Biggs had me write down the Bible verses she wanted for her funeral. And the psalms. And the hymns. She told me the names of flowers she hoped to have on her grave if she died this summer. And which ones she wanted should she last until fall, which she thought unlikely. I felt sad that she was so alone. That she had to tell her last wishes to a strange girl who had come to her by accident.

Then I heard footsteps. A woman about Aunt Margaret's age came into the cabin. She said, "Mother! Not again!"

Mrs. Biggs's daughter turned to me. She said, "I suppose Sally brought you."

I said she had.

"And did you write a list of Mother's last wishes?" she asked.

I nodded. Had she been peeking at the window?

Mrs. Biggs's daughter told me that her mother has sold Sally four times. Each time, Sally has brought a child back to this cabin. Each time, her mother asked the child to write down her last wishes. She said that her mother was as healthy as a horse. She said her mother would outlive us all.

Mrs. Biggs said she did not think she would last the night.

Mrs. Biggs's daughter gave me a biscuit. She told me that she has ten children. She begs her mother to come and live with her family. But Mrs. Biggs says no.

At dusk, Uncle Aubert rode up. When I did not come home, he guessed that Sally had gone back to her old barn. Mrs. Biggs gave him his money back, and we rode home double on Star.

July 19, 1856

Every part of me hurts from bouncing on Sally.

Lily came over today. I told her about Sally. Lily says she will find out if Honey has a brother or sister who could be my pony.

Lily and I braided prairie grass into a crown for Grace. Lily said I was lucky to have a little sister. She asked if I have been praying for her baby sister. Every night, I told her.

July 22, 1856

I was watering the apple trees this morning when I heard Mother scream. I quickly filled my bucket from the barrel and ran to the summer kitchen. I feared she had set something on fire. Aunt Margaret ran in from the cabin. But nothing was burning. Mother was pointing

at a black snake behind the stovepipe, yelling, "Kill it! Kill it!" Aunt Margaret said no. She said we are lucky to have this kind of snake. It will keep the kitchen free of rats. Mother sat down on a cracker box. She said she was weak in the knees.

July 25, 1856

We had a close call.

We were in the cabin yesterday, fixing midday dinner. We heard thunder. Aunt Margaret looked out the window. She said, "I don't like that sky." I looked out. The sky was glowing very bright. Aunt Margaret said heat lightning must have touched off a fire in the dry prairie grass. We ran outside. Uncle Aubert was hurrying out of the barn. He had seen the sky. He said the wind was blowing the fire our way!

John and Pres led Bay, Star, Mollie, and her calves down to the stream for safety. Charlie and Grace chased the chickens down, too. Aunt Margaret hitched Kip to the wagon. We ran him down to the stream with the water barrel, filled it, and ran him up the hill. When we got back, George had made three piles of prairie grass. Uncle Aubert was lighting them on fire! I thought he had lost his mind. But Aunt Margaret said he was lighting "back-fires." He wanted the little fires to burn up all the grass near the cabin. Then there would be nothing left for the big fire to burn.

The air grew hot and smoky. It was hard to breathe. Suddenly, orange flames burst out of the smoke! I was so scared.

Mother handed out flour sacks. We all dunked them in the water barrel. Pres stood on one side of me. George stood on the other. We slapped at the flames with the wet sacks.

When the sacks dried out, we dunked them again. Then we slapped at the flames some more. We fought that fire for hours. Perspiration poured off of us. We could hardly breathe for the smoke. I thought we might have to run down to the stream and save ourselves while the cabin burned.

Then, out of the gray smoke came the Vanbeeks' wagon. Lily's three big brothers jumped out. They had seen the flames and had come to help. They brought more flour sacks. They stood by us, battling the flames.

At last, Uncle Aubert called from somewhere in the smoke, "I think we got it beat!"

The flames near us grew smaller. In time, the wind blew the smoke away. The terrible fire was still burning out on the prairie. But it had not burned down our cabin. Or our barn.

Finally, we stopped slapping at the flames.

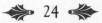 24

Only then did my arms begin to ache. We washed the black soot from our faces. When we looked at one another, we saw that our eyebrows and lashes had been burned off! Aunt Margaret says they will soon grow back.

July 28, 1856

We took carrots and potatoes to the Vanbeeks' cabin for a potluck supper. As we ate, Lily's oldest brother, Theo, talked to Uncle Aubert. He said more than a thousand Ruffians are hiding around Lawrence. He says they have rifles with knife-sharp bayonets attached to their barrels. I am frightened of Ruffians. I wish they would all go home.

After dinner, Lily helped her mother serve four more plates of food. Sam and William, Lily's other big brothers, took the plates and slipped outside. No one said a word. But I

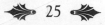

knew they were taking the food to the smokehouse. A family is hiding there. They are waiting for the Underground Railroad to take them north to freedom. If they are found, it would be awful. They would have to go back to slavery. And Mr. Vanbeek would go to jail.

July 31, 1856

Hot, hot, hot. Even the wind is hot. All but two of Mother's baby apple trees have died. The cabin smells of smoke from the fire. We are all eaten up by mosquitoes. Mother is so weak and thin. Father should have been here two weeks ago. Where is he?

I am a St. Louis girl. I will never be a prairie girl. Oh, how I long to go home!

August 1, 1856

Pres loves K.T. He even loves the black snake in the summer kitchen. He calls him Jake. He says Jake lets him pat his head.

Later

Uncle Aubert went into Lawrence today. He came home looking grim. After supper, he and Aunt Margaret walked out on the prairie by themselves. It is dark now. They have not come back. I write by the light of a candle set on the overturned wash-tub. Mother sits beside me, knitting a sweater for Father. I asked her what was wrong with Uncle Aubert. She said when he wants us to know, he will tell us.

August 5, 1856

Uncle Aubert gathered us together this morning before chores. He told us he is going off to fight with the Free-State Militia! He hugged us each in turn. Then he rode off on Star. We watched him go. Aunt Margaret said she is proud he is fighting for this land. Fighting so his family will grow up in a free state.

I am proud, too. But I hate to think of Uncle Aubert ducking down in a mud fort, so as not to be shot by Ruffians.

August 6, 1856

Theo Vanbeek rode over today. He had heard that Uncle Aubert went to fight with the Militia. He asked if there were any chores he might do. There were many! George was

out hunting. So Theo did his chores. Then h
split wood, hoed potatoes, and mended the
fence.

Before he left, Theo warned us that Ruffians
are raiding Free-State settler cabins. They steal
money, jewelry, and horses. Aunt Margaret
folded her arms. She said they will not be
stealing from us.

Later

Aunt Margaret hollowed out a log. I helped
her wrap up her silver brooch. And Uncle
Aubert's gold watch. We put them inside the
log. Aunt Margaret rolled up Uncle Aubert's
banknotes. She stuffed them into the log, too.
Then she plugged the log with wood at the
end. She put this log and two others into the
fireplace. The weather is so hot, we never use
the fireplace now. If the Ruffians come, Aunt

Margaret says they will never think to look inside a log.

Aunt Margaret came up with a plan to keep our horse safe, too. We made a big haystack behind the cabin. At dusk, Charlie led Bay into the narrow space between the haystack and our cabin. There, he is hidden from the view of any passing Ruffians. Charlie handed Bay's halter through the back window to Aunt Margaret. She tied it to her bedpost. She says she will sleep with a revolver under her pillow. If any horse thieves come, she will use it. If we are in the cabin when shooting starts, she says we are to drop to the floor. That is the safest place to be.

Mother says, "Lord help us all."

Later

George shot two prairie hens. It was my job to pluck their feathers. Then I helped Aunt Margaret cut them up. It was awful, bloody work. It made me wish I were a vegetarian, like Hannah Peach. I had such fun riding the steamboat to Kansas City with Hannah. I wonder how she likes living in the vegetarian community.

August 9, 1856

Late last night, I heard men shouting. Gunshots rang out. I was frightened! George heard me tossing. He lifted up the quilt and whispered to me not to worry. Ruffians are known to drink a great deal of whiskey, he said. In a while, the whiskey will put them to sleep. George was right. Before long, the

singing and shouting died down. The Ruffians fell asleep. So did I.

This morning, Aunt Margaret told George not to go hunting. The other boys are not to gather cow chips. She said we have enough water in the barrel. So I need not go down to the stream. Aunt Margaret told me to keep Grace close by the cabin. She put the cows and Kip on picket lines instead of letting them graze in the prairie. Everywhere she went today, even to the barn, she carried a rifle.

Mother stayed inside the cabin. The least noise makes her jump. She tried to knit. But her hands shook so that she had to stop.

We all are afraid. Even Mouser crouched down beside the cabin door all day. Is Uncle Aubert fighting the Ruffians? Where is Father? Oh, why can't we all go home to St. Louis?

August 10, 1856

Father is here! Mother is sobbing for joy. I am, too. I cannot write another word.

August 11, 1856

Father slept for a long time. Then he told us his story. He sold our St. Louis house, carriage, and horses to our next-door neighbor there. He sold his business, too. He arranged to have our furniture shipped to K.T. Then he packed two trunks with china, silver, and linen. He took them and boarded the steamboat *Belle*. The ship started up the Missouri River.

Near Kansas City, Ruffians rowed out and blocked the river. They forced the *Belle* to pull ashore. They took over the boat! A Ruffian spy had been aboard since St. Louis. The spy told

which passengers were Free-State men. He pointed out Father and some friends he had met on board. The Ruffians threw them off the boat. They had to leave their trunks behind. They were lucky to escape with their lives.

The Missouri–K.T. border is patrolled by Ruffians. They will not let Free-State men cross into K.T. So Father and his friends headed north to Nebraska. They hid by day. By night, they walked or caught rides on wagons. Then they came into K.T. from the north.

After Father told his story, Pres said, "Did the Ruffians steal everything?"

"Not everything," said Father. He surprised us by unbuttoning two of his shirt buttons. A money belt was tied around his middle. When he sold our house in St. Louis, he was paid in gold. He put the gold pieces in his money belt and hid it under his shirt. I am so glad the Ruffians did not get Father's gold!

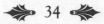

August 12, 1856

Uncle Aubert came home last night! He slipped into the cabin after dark. When we heard his voice, we all galloped down from the loft. Aunt Margaret hugged him. Mother fixed him a plate of prairie chicken. He ate it quickly. He must have been very hungry.

Uncle Aubert said that last week the Militia stormed a Ruffian fort. The Ruffians did not put up a fight. They ran off scared into the woods. They left behind many guns and boxes of ammunition. Now these things are the property of the Free-State Militia. The Ruffians left behind whiskey bottles, too. But they were all empty.

Uncle Aubert asked if we would like to help in the fight for a free Kansas.

"Yes!" we all said. "How can we help?"

Uncle Aubert said that the Militia has

lookouts on top of Blue Mound. If they see Ruffians marching for Lawrence at night, they will light a big fire. This will signal the Militia in Lawrence to get ready for a battle. If the Ruffians come by day, the lookouts will signal by raising a flag. A tall pine tree has been cut down for a flagpole. Brass rings have been attached to the top. A hole has been dug for the pole.

"But we do not have a flag," said Uncle Aubert. "Can you sew a flag for the Free-State Militia?"

Aunt Margaret, Mother, and I said, "Yes!"

The boys looked disappointed. I think they hoped for a more exciting way to help the Militia than sewing.

Uncle Aubert said the flag must be big. Big enough to be seen five miles away in Lawrence.

"We can use my bedsheet," said Mother.

I was ready to start sewing right then, by candlelight. But Aunt Margaret says we will wait for daylight. Uncle Aubert says he will come back in three nights to get the flag.

Father and Uncle Aubert stayed up late, talking.

August 13, 1856

The most awful thing has happened. I woke up this morning and Father was gone! He went with Uncle Aubert to fight with the Free-State Militia.

I cried so hard when Mother told me. Father has been in Kansas only three days. Why should he fight for this land? I know it is wrong, but I hate the prairie. I hate K.T.

Later

When we work on our flag, I forget to worry. Aunt Margaret found two yards of red calico. Charlie drew lines on it. He cut it into wide strips. Pres and John pinned the calico strips onto the bedsheet. They are not straight. But it does not matter. The important thing is that the flag can be seen in Lawrence.

Aunt Margaret said it would not do to have one side of our flag look like a white flag of surrender. So we are sewing bold red stripes onto both sides of the bedsheet. It is so big that we can all stitch on it at once. Aunt Margaret and I each took an edge. Mother took an edge, too. But her hands shook too much to sew.

Bedtime

I hear guns firing in the distance. I pray that Father and Uncle Aubert are safe.

August 14, 1856

Mother stayed in bed this morning. Aunt Margaret says she has a touch of the ague, also known as the "K.T. shakes." She is so hot. I sponged her forehead with cool water to bring down her fever.

I am trying not to worry.

Later

Father has never fired a rifle. Now he is off fighting a war. Mother has a terrible fever. She shakes so hard her teeth rattle. I am so afraid!

Aunt Margaret says I must think on the good. And here is something good. With the war and sickness, Mother will never want to live in K.T. Surely when the war is over, we will go home!

Later

We sewed strings along one edge of the flag. Now it can be tied to a rope. Our flag is finished.

August 15, 1856

Uncle Aubert did not come last night.

Mother is still fevered. Grace and Pres take turns bringing me cool cloths to bathe her face. It does them good to feel they are helping.

Later

I helped George make bullets. We melted lead in a small pan over a fire. We poured the melted lead into twelve small molds. When the lead cooled, we snapped the molds apart and pried out twelve hard lead bullets. We made 120 in all. Aunt Margaret says when Uncle Aubert comes for the flag, we will also give him bullets for his rifle.

August 16, 1856

Uncle Aubert has not come. George wants to take the flag to Blue Mound himself. He says the lookout cannot give the signal without it. But Aunt Margaret says it is too dangerous for him to go.

Later

Mother's fever has broken! She got up and hugged us. Then she went back to bed. But Aunt Margaret says she is on the mend.

August 18, 1856

George is gone! We awoke this morning and found a note on the breadboard. He has taken the flag to Blue Mound.

Aunt Margaret says George is smart. And careful. He will soon be home. Pres is stamping around the cabin. He is mad that George did not ask him to go along. Mother says it is just as well.

August 19, 1856

George came back this afternoon. Aunt Margaret held him close. She never said a word about how he disobeyed.

When we were out in the barn doing chores, George told us of his adventure. He left our cabin in the dark. Whenever he heard horses coming, he lay down and hid in the prairie grass. At dawn he reached the top of Blue Mound. He saw one man sitting beside a low campfire. George called out to him. The man was so startled he nearly shot George! The man said his name was Silas Ogden. The Militia needed all able men to fight. So Mr. Ogden was the only lookout on Blue Mound and was very jumpy. George gave him the flag. But Mr. Ogden only said, "How can I plant a dag-blasted flagpole all by my dag-blasted self?"

Mr. Ogden told George to skedaddle. So George came home.

Pres looked disappointed with George's story. I think he expected many soldiers and great rejoicing when his flag arrived on Blue Mound.

August 22, 1856

Theo Vanbeek came to do chores again. He brought us melons from his family's garden. He helped me take Kip down to the stream to fill the water barrel. As we went, I asked if his father was fighting with the Militia. Theo said no. I asked whether he or his brothers were going to fight. He said no. Why, I asked, was no one in his family fighting for a free Kansas? Theo said his family is of the Quaker faith. They do not believe in slavery. But they do not believe in fighting, either.

 44

"But that is not fair!" I said. "My father is fighting. My uncle is fighting. They may be shot! But they are fighting for this land to be free."

"Your father and uncle are doing what they think is right," Theo said. "And we are doing what we think is right. We do not believe in fighting wars."

After that, Theo and I emptied our buckets in silence.

Later

Tonight we ate the melons Theo brought. I did not like their taste.

August 24, 1856

After early chores, Mother opened the Bible for worship in our cabin. But Aunt Margaret

said she would go crazy with cabin fever if she did not get out. So we are going to the Blue Mound Sabbath School! Aunt Margaret said she will pray that the Ruffians will not be so coldhearted as to attack a wagon full of women and children on their way to church.

Later

I put on my cream silk dress for Sabbath School. How good it felt to be dressed like my old, St. Louis self again! Mother helped Pres into his St. Louis clothes, too. He fussed the whole time. Grace would not take off her prairie dress. George hitched up the wagon and we drove to Blue Mound. We passed Mrs. Biggs's cabin on the way. I thought that by now she had most likely gone to her heavenly reward.

We reached Blue Mound. We walked partway up it, to a clearing. We sat on logs in a semicircle. I counted twenty-two other children at the Sabbath School. We sang hymns. Then a Reverend Still told us the story of Daniel in the lion's den. He said Daniel was in terrible danger. But his faith kept him safe. After the story, I prayed for faith that would keep Father safe. I prayed so hard I forgot I was sitting on a log, and I rolled off backward. Pres laughed so hard that he nearly rolled off, too. I only hope most folks were praying with their eyes closed and did not see me with my feet up in the air.

After Sabbath School, Pres begged to run to the top of Blue Mound to see the "dag-blasted" lookout. Mother said, "Preston! Language!"

August 27, 1856

Mr. Young, the traveling photographer, came by this evening. Mother and Aunt Margaret fixed him a plate. The three of them

 47

whispered together. I heard Mr. Young say that more and more Ruffians are coming into K.T. They plan to attack Lawrence!

Later

Mr. Young showed us a photograph of a big cannon called Old Sacramento. It belongs to the Free-State Militia. But the Ruffians stole it. They took it to Franklin, a town not far from Lawrence. A Free-State spy went to Franklin. He found the house where the cannon was hidden. He said the Ruffians were always in that house, guarding Old Sacramento.

The Free-State men thought up a plan to get the cannon back. They loaded a wagon with hay. They drove it to the front door of the house. They rammed open the front door with a log, set fire to the hay, and pushed the wagon into the house. Thinking the house was on

 48

fire, the Ruffians ran out the back door. The Free-State men quickly put out the fire. Then they rushed inside to get their cannon. At first, they did not see it. Then they spotted it, standing in a corner of the dining room with its muzzle up, dressed as a woman!

Pres laughed so hard at this he got the hiccups.

August 29, 1856

As Mr. Young was leaving, Pres ran out of the summer kitchen. Jake the snake was coiled around his arm! I think he hoped to scare Mr. Young. But Mr. Young asked to take a picture of Pres and his snake.

Mr. Young put a shiny copperplate into his camera. He had Pres sit on an overturned bucket. He told him to look at the camera and hold very still. He asked me to count slowly to

fifteen. Pres held up the arm with Jake wrapped around it. He stared at the camera. Jake stared at the camera, too.

Mr. Young said, "Count!"

And I began, "One . . . two . . . three . . ."

Press held still. So did Jake. I kept counting, "Six . . . seven . . ."

Suddenly Jake's head darted over to the left. Pres did not move. So I kept counting. At last I said, "Fifteen!"

Mr. Young said, "Got it!"

He took the copperplate out of his camera. He dipped it into a funny-smelling liquid. Slowly Pres's likeness began to appear on the plate. Mr. Young washed the plate with water. He laid it out to dry.

As it dried, Pres looked at it and cried, "Jake has two heads!"

I looked at the copperplate. It was true!

Mr. Young laughed. He said it was because Jake had moved while the photograph was being taken.

When the plate was dry, Mr. Young put it into a viewing box. He said he would call it "Boy with a Two-Headed Snake." He gave the box to Pres. I have never seen my brother so happy.

August 30, 1856

Aunt Margaret stepped in a prairie-dog hole and sprained her ankle! She called for George and Charlie, and they helped her hobble back to the cabin. They sat her up in bed. Mother was close to tears. But Aunt Margaret laughed. She said her ankle looked like a melon. How can she be cheerful even now?

Later

It turned suddenly cold last night.

Theo Vanbeek rode over to see about chores. We were glad to see him. With the men away, Aunt Margaret lame, and Mother so weak, it is hard to get the chores done. Theo hauled wood, split it, pitched hay, and mended Bay's harness. But I still think he is awful for not fighting for a free Kansas.

September 2, 1856

After supper tonight, three wagons pulled up to our cabin. They were full of children and their mothers. One mother said, "Please, may we stay with you this night?" She said a man rode into Lawrence shouting that the Ruffians were coming to burn the town! There are not enough men in Lawrence to protect everyone.

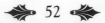

So the men sent the women and children to stay at the farms for safety.

"Come in," said Mother. "We will find a place for everyone to sleep."

Pres and John are making prairie feather beds in the barn. The boys will sleep there. Mother will share her bed with another mother. Aunt Margaret will share her big bed with two. We girls will sleep up in the loft. We took down the blue-and-white quilt. We pushed the beds together to make three big beds. We will sleep crosswise, five to a bed. It is chilly. I must find more quilts. No more time to write now!

Later

Two of the Lawrence girls, Louisa and India, are nine. Just my age! Before the war, they went to school in Lawrence. They have also read *The Tempest* by Mr. Shakespeare. Go

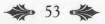

home, Ruffians! If only I could go to school, maybe K.T. would not be so bad.

September 3, 1856

George got up before dawn to take care of the animals. It was a frosty morning. So he lit a fire to warm the cabin.

I came down the loft ladder just as Aunt Margaret hobbled out of her quilt room. She saw the fire burning. Her eyes grew wide. Then I remembered. Her jewelry and money! They were inside the hollowed-out log! The fire was blazing hot. Aunt Margaret poured water on it. But it was too late. When the fire was finally out, Aunt Margaret pulled out two black lumps from the ashes. One was her silver brooch. The other was Uncle Aubert's gold watch. She found the roll of banknotes, too. It was so badly burned that she could not unroll it.

Poor George! He was near tears at having burned his family's few riches. He was out hunting when Aunt Margaret hollowed out that log. No one thought to tell him about it. Aunt Margaret hugged him. She says she will mail the burned money to the government in Washington. It will show them what happens to banknotes out here in the wilds of K.T.

Later

Mother and I made johnnycakes for breakfast. We fed the children in shifts. Then the older children helped us with our chores. The little ones played with Mouser near the cabin. When it got warm, we all went down to the stream. As we waded, India told me her father had once bought Sally from Mrs. Biggs!

About midday, a man rode to our cabin. He said the news about the raid was a false alarm.

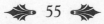

So all the mothers and children piled into the wagons and went back to town.

Our cabin seems empty now with only eight of us. Mother is revived by caring for so many children.

September 12, 1856

Mr. Young rode by our cabin. He says the President has sent a new governor to K.T. He is Governor Geary and he wants to end the war! He has ordered all Ruffians to go home. If they do not obey, he will call out United States soldiers to drive them out of K.T. Mr. Young says peace is at hand. Aunt Margaret wept with joy.

Mr. Young told us another story about Old Sacramento. He reminded us how the Ruffians threw thousands of lead newspaper-type letters

from *The Herald of Freedom* into the river. He said Free-State men raked much of the type out of the river. They melted the lead letters, just the way George and I melted lead to make bullets. They poured the melted lead into big round molds to make cannonballs.

Pres whooped when he heard this.

The men loaded up Old Sacramento with these cannonballs. And they fired the cannon at a Ruffian fort. The man who lit the cannon cried out, "Another issue of *The Herald of Freedom*!"

We all whooped when we heard this.

Old Sacramento is in Lawrence now. Mr. Young says if we hear it boom, it will be a signal. We are quickly to pack up what we can and go hide in the woods behind Blue Mound.

Mr. Young left to tell others about the signal.

September 13, 1856

Aunt Margaret says we may go to Sabbath School tomorrow! She says Governor Geary has sent the Ruffians home. She says it will be safe to go.

September 14, 1856

The Ruffians did NOT go home. I am sitting at the foot of Blue Mound now. Here is what happened.

We drove the wagon to Blue Mound. We walked to Reverend Still's cabin. But no one was there. We saw two women standing halfway up Blue Mound. Aunt Margaret stayed in the wagon with her boys. Mother, Grace, Pres, and I walked up the hill to the women. One was looking through a spyglass. Mother asked her what she saw. She handed the spyglass to

Mother. Mother looked through it and said, "Good heavens!" Pres grabbed for the spyglass, but I got it first. I put it to my eye. I saw something shiny. It took me a moment to understand. I was looking at thousands of bayonets sparkling in the sunlight. Each one was fastened to the barrel of a Ruffian rifle!

"They are fifteen miles away," said one woman.

"And marching this way," said the other.

"Has anyone raised the flag on top of Blue Mound?" asked Pres.

The women did not know about any flag. They said they were going home to bury their silver and hide their cows.

Before Mother could stop him, Pres began running up Blue Mound. Mother held tight to Grace's hand. She said, "Go after your brother, Meg."

I took off running. When I got to the top of

Blue Mound, I saw a soldier. I knew he must be Silas Ogden. Pres was trying to help him plant the pine-tree flagpole in the hole. But the pole was too heavy.

"I will get the others!" I shouted to Pres.

I turned and started running back down the mound.

Mr. Ogden shouted after me, "And bring a dag-blasted rope!"

I ran to Mother. I said Pres and Mr. Ogden needed help. Then we raced down the hill.

Two minutes later, George, Charlie, and John were speeding up Blue Mound.

Mother sat down in the wagon. Her face was flushed. She was shaking again. I ran to Reverend Still's barn for a rope. The horses and cows were gone. I looked everywhere for a rope. But wherever Reverend Still had gone, he had taken his rope with him.

I ran back to the wagon. Mother said we must ride home for a rope. But I said, "Wait! We can look in Mrs. Biggs's barn."

Off we drove. Aunt Margaret pulled the wagon up to Mrs. Biggs's barn. I raced inside. I found a rope. But it was too short to raise a flag.

I ran out of the barn. Someone called, "Stop, thief!" Mrs. Biggs stood on her cabin steps. She had not gone to her heavenly reward. She held a rifle!

"You are too late!" Mrs. Biggs cried. "My pony is already stolen!"

"Sally?" I said. "The Ruffians stole Sally?"

Now Mrs. Biggs seemed to remember me. She lowered her gun.

In a rush of words, I told her how we needed a rope to raise the flag. Mrs. Biggs shook her head. My heart sank. Now we would have to ride all the way home. We might be too late!

Then Mrs. Biggs said, "My bed cord will do."

With that, she hurried into the cabin quicker than one would think a dying woman could. I ran after her. I helped her push her mattress onto the floor. A long cord was threaded up and down and back and forth through holes in the wooden bed frame. Our fingers flew as we began untying knots. Soon I held the cord in my arms. I thanked Mrs. Biggs and ran for the door.

It wasn't long before I was running up Blue Mountain again. Grace was with me now. Mother ran behind us. By the time we reached the top, Mr. Ogden and the boys had planted the flagpole. Now Pres shinnied up the pole. Mr. Ogden tossed him one end of the cord. Pres threaded it through the rings at the top of the pole. He slid down the pole again. We tied our flag to the cord. Then Mr. Ogden pulled on

the cord and raised our flag. How proud we felt! Our flag was waving over Blue Mound! Mr. Ogden said it was the best dag-blasted flag he had ever seen.

A minute later, we heard a cannon boom. Old Sacramento! We knew our flag had done its job.

We hurried down the hill. But Aunt Margaret and the wagon were gone. And that is all I know.

Later

We are still sitting at the foot of Blue Mound. Aunt Margaret has not come back. Now Pres is shouting. Aunt Margaret is coming! He says Kip and Mollie and the calves are with her. And some old lady, too. What is going on?

September 16, 1856

Mr. Young spread the word about the signal. Everyone for miles around heard Old Sacramento boom. Mothers gathered up their children. They gathered up their animals, too. Cows, horses, oxen, dogs, and cats. And chickens. We are all hiding together in the thick woods behind Blue Mound.

Aunt Margaret had gone back to get our animals. And she picked up Mrs. Biggs. She brought her to hide behind Blue Mound. George and Charlie helped Aunt Margaret hobble to our encampment with her swollen ankle. I helped Mrs. Biggs. Grace carried Mouser. Now Pres is running around, pulling up his pant leg. He proudly shows off the splinters he got sliding down the flagpole to anyone who will look.

Lily is here with her whole family. Her

father and brothers are the only men he. They are making themselves useful chopping wood for campfires. How ashamed Lily must be that they are not off fighting.

When I went for water, I passed Mrs. Biggs's daughter and her ten children. I told Mrs. Biggs I would take her to their camp. But she said she liked our camp just fine.

India and Louisa are here, too. At times we forget that we are here because the Ruffians are coming. At times it feels more like a picnic. But most of the time we are all sick with worry for our fathers. We hear that two thousand Ruffian soldiers are marching toward Lawrence. George says there are only three hundred men in the Free-State Militia. How do they stand a chance?

Everyone here says Governor Geary is no better than a Ruffian himself. He made us feel safe when the Ruffians were coming!

What a night! We were asleep in the woods. A terrible boom woke us. The Ruffians! Were they shooting at us? Everyone leaped up. Children cried. Dogs barked. Horses whinnied. Mouser raced up a tree. Mothers called to their children. No one knew what was happening. Then a flash lit the sky. Another boom sounded and rain began to fall. It was only a thunderstorm! We all got soaked. Our bedding, too. But we all felt happy that no one was shooting at us.

The mothers herded us to Reverend Still's cabin. Poor Mrs. Still. She opened the door and there we were. Dozens of children, dripping wet and muddy. But she let us in. She gave out rags and we dried ourselves as best we could. Then we lay down on her rag rug. Keeping together for warmth, we fell asleep.

This morning the sun is out. The little children ran outside. Lily and I stayed behind to clean the mud out of the Still's cabin. As we worked, Lily asked if I had been praying for her sister. With Father off fighting, I said, all my prayers are for him. Lily was quiet then. Now I wonder, is she upset that I have not been praying for her sister? Or that her father did not go off to fight?

Later

Mr. Young came to our camp. He said Governor Geary went to Franklin. He told the Ruffians to go home. He said if they did not go, he would call out the U.S. soldiers. We have heard this before. We do not believe Governor Geary wants the Ruffians to go home.

September 18, 1856

Mother shook us awake before dawn. She said we must run. And quickly! "Ruffian soldiers are on top of Mount Oread," she said. "Get up! Hurry!"

We jumped up. We grabbed our bedding. Everyone in the woods was doing the same. We kept quiet. No one wanted to let the Ruffians know we were there. We rounded up Kip, Mollie, and the calves.

George was hitching up Bay when a shout went up. My heart nearly stopped. Theo Vanbeek came tearing down Blue Mound. He yelled, "The soldiers on Mount Oread are United States troops! They have come to chase the Ruffians home!"

Never have I heard such whooping.

Later

We do not know if it is safe to go back to our cabins yet. So we are waiting at the foot of Blue Mound. I am looking after Grace. Grace is looking after Mouser. Pres is still showing off his splinters.

I still want to go back to St. Louis. But life here in K.T. certainly is exciting.

Later

Theo Vanbeek rode by to say the area is free of Ruffians. We are going home!

Later

We took Mrs. Biggs home first. I helped her into her cabin. I saw her mattress on the floor.

69

Her bed cord! It was still on the flagpole. But Mrs. Biggs said never mind. She could sleep on the floor. She said a dying woman does not care much for comfort.

I am writing in the wagon now. We are going home!

Later

The Ruffians broke into our cabin! As we rode up to it, we saw the door standing open. And we knew. All the bedding Aunt Margaret did not take to Blue Mound is gone. So are Uncle Aubert's hammer and hatchet. Every scrap of food is gone. And Uncle Aubert's whiskey bottle. The Ruffians took what was growing in the garden, too. But Aunt Margaret is smiling. She says we are all alive and unhurt. And so are Kip, Bay, and Mollie and her calves. She had hidden the chickens in the cellar. She

says we have more flour in the cellar, too. And potatoes. She says we can stitch new quilts. She says if the Ruffians are leaving K.T. looting and stealing, so be it. At least they are leaving. Now Father and Uncle Aubert can come home!

Later

Pres ran into the cabin yelling that Jake did not come out from behind the stovepipe. He says the Ruffians took his snake. Mother says this is doubtful.

September 22, 1856

Father is wounded! Shot in the shoulder. Two Free-State men drove him to our cabin last night. They said he was shot yesterday when the Militia attacked a Ruffian fort.

 71

Father lay in the back of the wagon. His eyes were closed. Blood was all over his shirt. Now he is sleeping in the big bed. Mother cleaned his wound. She says the bullet is still lodged in his shoulder.

I cried when I saw Father. Aunt Margaret held me in her arms. She told me to think on the good. But all I can think is how good it will be when we go back home.

September 23, 1856

I tiptoed into Father's room this morning. He lay so still. I squeezed his hand. And he squeezed back! Now I know he will get well.

Later

Father opened his eyes this evening. Mother managed to get a little soup into him before he fell asleep. Mother is like her old self again.

Where is Uncle Aubert?

September 24, 1856

Aunt Margaret and George have gone to look for Uncle Aubert. They hitched Bay to the wagon this morning and rode off. Mother is busy tending Father. I gathered Charlie, John, Pres, and Grace together. I said we must do all the work now. Pres said, "We'll do a dag-blasted good job!" And we did. Charlie and John looked after the animals. Pres and Grace cleaned up the garden. They found carrots and squash that the Ruffians left behind. I cooked them for supper. No one complained.

Later

Father sat up today. He said he last saw Uncle Aubert at the Ruffian fort. He does not know where he is now. Father has dark circles under his eyes.

Jake the snake came out from behind the stovepipe. Pres wants to show him to Father. He says it will cheer him. Mother says not yet.

Later

Aunt Margaret and George came home just after dark. They found Uncle Aubert. He is alive. But he is in prison! He is being held with twenty other Free-State soldiers. Governor Geary had sent them north to stop the Ruffians from looting and stealing. On their way back to Lawrence, Uncle Aubert and the others were captured by pro-slavery soldiers. They took them to Lecompton and locked them in jail. The men were brought before Judge Cato. He is a pro-slavery man. He said he would not set bail for any men of the Free-State Militia. So they are still in jail. And all their horses, including Star, have been taken by pro-slavery men. Mother says this is robbery.

Aunt Margaret says she is only happy that she found Uncle Aubert alive.

September 27, 1856

The Emigrant Aid Society in Boston has sent barrels to Lawrence. Theo Vanbeek brought one to our cabin on the back of his wagon. When I saw it, I feared the whole thing might be filled with boys' shoes. Aunt Margaret opened the barrel. Inside were boys' shoes. And girls' shoes. And warm woolen shawls, sweaters, pants, dresses, and socks. On the very bottom

of the barrel were three fancy dresses. The kind I wore in St. Louis. I held up a pale blue one in front of me. It is just my size. A St. Louis dress! It has a high lacy collar. And twenty-one buttons down the back. It made me think of Nellie, fastening my buttons with a buttonhook. Dear Nellie! I wonder if she is married now to Mr. Sean O'Brien.

Mother said these clothes are to be given to the needy. I said I was in need of the blue dress. Mother said I could pick one dress from the barrel. But I must be practical. For this is the only dress I will get this year. She held up a brown wool dress. It is a fine dress for some prairie girl. But I am a St. Louis girl. I have my heart set on that blue St. Louis dress.

September 30, 1856

I went with Aunt Margaret to give away the clothes from the barrel. It was frosty out. We covered up with a buffalo lap robe and drove east. We stopped at a cabin built into the side of a hill. Aunt Margaret called it a "soddy." Its roof was grass. A woman asked us in. The soddy was dark inside. And damp. The ceiling was packed dirt. And tree roots. I saw a little snake winding its way through the roots. Pres might like to live in a soddy.

Two children sat at a table eating soup. I helped their mother pick warm winter clothing for them.

As we were leaving, a child cried out. I looked back and saw that the little snake had fallen into her soup!

We went to six more soddies. People took wool sweaters and shawls from the barrel.

They took wool pants and socks. But nobody took the St. Louis dress.

When we got home, Aunt Margaret said, "I guess it is yours, Meg."

I put it on. It fits perfectly!

Later

Mother did not eat much supper tonight. She is worried. Father's wound is not healing.

October 1, 1856

Father has a fever. His wound is festering. Aunt Margaret mixed herbs with hot water. She wrapped them in a rag. She put this compress on Father's wound to draw out the infection. I hope this will help him!

October 3, 1856

Father did not wake up all day yesterday. Mother is beside herself with worry. This is worse than cholera. I want to go home!

October 4, 1856

Father has not eaten in two days. George has driven Aunt Margaret to Blue Mound to get Reverend Still. He is a doctor as well as a preacher. Aunt Margaret says he will know how to help Father.

Later

Aunt Margaret came back without Reverend Still. He was not at home. Mrs. Still says he went off to help the Free-State Militia. Now who will help Father?

Oh, Lord, please help Father get better. Please, please, help him get well!

October 6, 1856

A miracle has happened!

Father was sleeping. The rest of us sat around the fire. The boys were mending harnesses. Mother, Aunt Margaret, and I were stitching to keep ourselves from worrying. We heard the sound of a wagon coming. Aunt Margaret hobbled to the window. She picked up the rifle she keeps in the corner. "Get down," she said.

I flattened myself on the floor. Mother rushed in to Father.

I heard the wagon coming closer. My heart was pounding. Were Ruffians coming to burn our cabin?

Aunt Margaret aimed the rifle.

Then I heard someone call, "Whoa, Ruby! Whoa, Blanco!"

I jumped up, shouting, "Don't shoot! It is Dr. Baer!"

We all ran outside. And there were Dr. Baer, Miss Peach, and Hannah Peach!

When Mother saw Dr. Baer, tears sprang to her eyes. He had been a dear friend in St. Louis. His wife and daughters died of cholera. So he decided to move to Kansas. Mother took Dr. Baer's hand and led him in to see Father. Dr. Baer gave him some medicine. Tomorrow when he has good light, Dr. Baer says he will take the bullet out of Father's shoulder.

Aunt Margaret offered to warm up some of our beef stew for Dr. Baer and the Peaches. But they are vegetarians and eat no meat. So they had only biscuits for supper.

Even by the light of one candle I could see that Hannah Peach has lost her rosy cheeks.

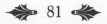

81

She has lost weight, too. So have Miss Peach and our dear "old Bear." When I heard their story, I understood why.

When we were on the steamboat, Dr. Baer and the Peaches showed Pres and me a pamphlet. It was from a vegetarian community in Neosho, K.T. The pamphlet had pictures of fine houses. And a flour mill on a river. Dr. Baer and the Peaches sent money to buy land in Neosho. Now Dr. Baer told us it was a bogus pamphlet. When they got to Neosho, they found nothing. No houses. No flour mill. No river. There was only rocky ground. And the deserted cabins of other vegetarians who had left Neosho. Or sickened and died.

Hannah stood before the fire, warming her poor red hands. Miss Peach told us that several times a day, Hannah walked a mile to a stream for water. She carried a yoke on her shoulders

with a bucket on each end, like an ox. Poor Hannah Peach!

The boys brought in hay and made prairie feather beds for Dr. Baer and the Peaches.

Mother says her prayers have been answered. Mine have, too.

October 7, 1856

Soon after sunup, Dr. Baer got his bag. He asked Aunt Margaret to get the whiskey. But there is no whiskey. The Ruffians stole it. Now Father will have nothing to ease his pain.

Dr. Baer went in to Father. Mother and Aunt Margaret went in to help. I heard Dr. Baer talking. Then I heard Father scream. I ran from the cabin.

I am sitting in the prairie grass now. I am not at all brave. I could not stand Father's

screams. But I know good Dr. Baer will take good care of Father. I am thinking on the good. Good, good, good, good.

Later

I am holding a bullet in my hand. Dr. Baer took it out of Father's shoulder. He says now Father's wound will heal.

I remember the day George and I made bullets. Then, I did not know what one small bullet could do. This little lump of lead nearly killed my father. Did the bullets I made kill anyone? I will never know. But I will never make another one as long as I live.

October 10, 1856

Father is better! He is sitting up. He is eating soup and asking for more.

The rest of us have been working to bring in the wheat. Theo, Sam, and William Vanbeek came to help. We gathered the sheaves together and tied them into bundles. It is hard, hard work.

October 13, 1856

Today we dug ten bushels of potatoes out of the ground. Our fingers turned blue from the cold.

October 15, 1856

First frost last night. We got the wheat and potatoes in just in time!

 85

The boys moved the cookstove back into the cabin. Pres wanted to move Jake into the cabin, too. Mother said Jake is happy right where he is.

October 16, 1856

Father got out of bed today. He sat in the rocker. Dr. Baer made a sling for his arm. He says Father is on the mend.

Mother let Pres show Jake to Father. Father said he was quite a snake. Then Pres showed Father "Boy with a Two-Headed Snake." For the first time since he was brought home in the wagon, Father laughed. Pres said he knew Jake would cheer Father.

Aunt Margaret takes food to Uncle Aubert in prison when she can. The trial date for the Free-State prisoners is set. It will be on the last

day court is in session. We are all on pins and needles, hoping the judge will free the prisoners.

Bedtime

I still pray for Father's health. And for Uncle Aubert in prison. But now I can spare some prayers for Lily's baby sister.

October 22, 1856

George, Charlie, John, Pres, Grace, and I rode to Lecompton with Aunt Margaret. We went for Uncle Aubert's trial. Aunt Margaret asked us to go. She wanted to show the judge what a fine family Uncle Aubert has waiting for him back home. Mother put my hair in French braids. I put on my blue St. Louis dress. The boys got slicked up, too. It was cold.

So we bundled under the buffalo robe for the ride.

We reached Lecompton. We saw men standing around the cabin used for a courthouse. Some had on Free-State Militia uniforms. Mr. Young was there, taking photographs.

Aunt Margaret pointed out a man with a red scarf tied around his neck. She said he was Jim Lane, leader of the Free-State Militia. He came over to us. He looked angry. He told Aunt Margaret that Judge Cato did not come to court today. Jim Lane said it is a pro-slavery man's trick. Now the trial must be put off until spring. Now Uncle Aubert will be in prison all winter long!

Mr. Young came over to us, too. He said how sorry he was. Then he said as long as we were here, he would like to take our photograph. Aunt Margaret agreed. She says she will give Uncle Aubert the likenesses of his children for Christmas.

Mr. Young lined us up in two rows. I stood at the end in the second row. Pres stood in front of me.

"Hold still!" called Mr. Young. He began to count, "One . . . two . . . three . . ."

When Mr. Young said, "Seven!" Pres darted out of his place. He ran around back of everyone to the other side of the first row. Then he stood still.

Mr. Young counted, "Fourteen . . . fifteen! Got it!"

"Pres! What in the world?" said Aunt Margaret.

"You will see," said Mr. Young. He winked at Pres. He promised to bring the likeness by our cabin soon.

We were all quiet riding home.

I was glad to take off my St. Louis dress. I forgot how a lace-trimmed collar can itch.

November 3, 1856

The land office in Lecompton is open again. Dr. Baer and Miss Peach drove in and staked claims. Now they both own plots of land some six miles east of here.

November 4, 1856

Mr. Young stopped by. He gave Aunt Margaret the photograph he took of us in Lecompton.

"I call it 'Twins in the Family,'" he said.

We all looked at the photograph. Pres

stood at one end of the first row. And Pr
stood on the other end of the first row, too.

"Oh, Preston!" said Mother. "You have
ruined the picture!"

But Aunt Margaret laughed. She said seeing
the Pres twins would cheer Uncle Aubert no
end. She said he is a man in need of cheer.

November 7, 1856

Governor Geary has toured K.T. He says it
is free of Ruffians. Now we are truly at peace.
He has named November twentieth as a day of
Thanksgiving in K.T. We have lived through a
terrible time. Now we will have a day to give
thanks and count our blessings.

Theo Vanbeek came to help with chores. I am still angry at him. But when Hannah Peach saw him, roses came back into her cheeks. Wait until I tell Lily!

November 8, 1856

Mother and Aunt Margaret are organizing a big Thanksgiving dinner in Lawrence. They will sell tickets for two dollars each! That is a lot to pay for a dinner. But the money will go to buy bedding and warm winter clothing for the Lecompton prisoners. After the dinner there will be music and dancing. Pres and John are making the tickets. Mother says we will cook up a storm.

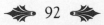

Later

Lily rode Honey over today. The Peaches had gone to their claim. So Hannah was not here. But I told Lily about her. And how her face turned pink when she spoke to Theo. Lily says we must get Theo to ask Hannah to dance at the Thanksgiving dinner.

I told Lily I have been praying for her sister. She was happy to hear it.

Then Lily and I had the best idea! We asked Mother if we could ride to the neighbors' cabins to sell Thanksgiving dinner tickets. She said yes!

November 10, 1856

George hitched Bay to the wagon. I drove to Lily's house. She sat beside me on the wagon seat as we drove from neighbor to

ighbor. Everyone bought tickets. Some paid with little gold dollars. Some with banknotes. Lily kept all the money in her pocket.

Our last stop was Mrs. Biggs's cabin. I feared that by now, she must surely have gone to her heavenly reward. But she was sitting on her porch. She told us that Sally had found her way home!

We asked Mrs. Biggs if she would like to buy a Thanksgiving dinner ticket. She said two dollars was a fortune. She said she would probably not last until Thanksgiving. But then she said she would not need money where she was going. So she might as well buy herself a ticket. She also bought a ticket for her daughter. And one for her daughter's husband. And ten more for all her ten grandchildren!

We drove home with sixty-four dollars. Lily said carrying so much money made her feel dizzy.

November 11, 1856

Mr. Vanbeek came to see about chores today. He and Father talked for a long time. When Mr. Vanbeek left, I went to sit beside Father. I said he must be angry with Mr. Vanbeek and his sons for not fighting for a free K.T. But Father surprised me. He said he thought Mr. Vanbeek was brave not to fight in the war.

I could not believe my ears!

"But you fought!" I said. "You almost died for this land." But Father said that if only everyone believed as the Vanbeeks did, there would be no war at all.

I will have to think on this. Maybe Theo and his family have the right idea after all.

November 12, 1856

Mother and Father drove into Lawrence today. They brought back a package from the post office for Aunt Margaret. She opened it and said, "I'll be!" She held up a stack of banknotes. The government in Washington sent them to her to replace the roll of burned money. George whooped for joy. Aunt Margaret says maybe some day paper money will catch on after all.

Then Mother said she had a surprise. She told us that today she and Father staked a claim for land two miles north of here. Father said in the spring, we will build a cabin.

Everyone whooped and cheered. Everyone but me. I cannot quite believe it. We will not be going home to St. Louis after all.

November 20, 1856

More than one hundred people came to Thanksgiving dinner. Father was mended enough to come!

Mr. Young took a photograph of all of us sitting on benches at a long table made of boards. Nell and India were there. Mrs. Biggs came. Her daughter's whole family did, too. So did Mr. Silas Ogden. When all were seated, we held hands. We bowed our heads. A Reverend Hutchinson offered a prayer. He gave thanks for this time of peace in Kansas Territory.

Then we feasted on vegetable stews, roasted turkey, baked ham, chicken pie, and fixings.

After dinner, I helped clear plates. For a dying woman, Mrs. Biggs surely has a good appetite! While I cleared, others served pie. Then we had announcements. Miss Peach stood. She thanked Mother and Aunt Margaret

r putting on the dinner. Others stood. They said they hoped the Lecompton prisoners would soon be freed. Mother slipped Lily and me seconds on pie. It helped us last through the announcements. Theo Vanbeek stood. He announced that the Lawrence School would begin next week. Lily and I threw our arms around each other. School! We whooped with joy. Finally Mr. Silas Ogden stood. He said this was the best dag-blasted dinner he had ever eaten.

Mr. Vanbeek tuned up his fiddle. Aunt Margaret got out her tambourine. The music started and everyone began to dance. Theo walked right up to Hannah Peach. The next minute, the two of them had joined the dancing. Lily and I did not have to do a thing. We watched them dance. Lily asked if Hannah were a Quaker. I said she was a vegetarian. Lily said that in K.T. that might be close enough.

Bedtime

We will not be going home to St. Louis. I am still getting used to the idea. And when I think about it, how could we go home? Our house has been sold. And our carriage. Dear Nellie has moved to New York to marry Sean O'Brien. We can never go back to that St. Louis. So I am no longer a St. Louis girl.

And if we could go back? I would miss Aunt Margaret and her cheerful ways. I would miss Uncle Aubert. And my cousins. I would miss Lily. And her prayed-for sister. I would miss my walk with Kip to the stream each morning. I would miss Mollie's sweet cow's breath. I would miss sleeping next to Grace in the Blue Quilt Room. I would miss Hannah Peach. I would even miss Jake. And anyone who could miss a snake is surely a prairie girl.

Historical Note

In 1856, Kansas was a territory belonging to the United States. Franklin Pierce was president of the United States. Everyone knew that Kansas would soon become a state. But would it allow slavery? Or would it become a state where slavery was against the law? Most Northerners wanted Kansas to be a free state. Most Southerners wanted Kansas to allow slavery. Everyone felt strongly about slavery.

President Pierce did not want to take a stand on slavery. He did not want to anger voters in the North or the South. So he declared that Kansas Territory hold an election. He said that the citizens of K.T. should vote on what kind

of a state it should become. This solved President Pierce's problem. But it caused terrible problems for everyone in K.T.

At this time, only white men could vote. But which white men? New people arrived in K.T. every day. Some planned to stay and make K.T. a home. Others were just looking around.

Ferrying pro-slavery voters to Kansas.

Because so many people were arriving in K.T., some pro-slavery judges came up with a plan. They made a rule that if a man had lived

in K.T. for one hour, he could vote. After this, men from the South rode to K.T. Many of them were a rough sort. When they crossed the border into K.T., they were called Border Ruffians. Some Ruffians voted once in the K.T. election. Others voted many times! When the votes were counted, it was no surprise that K.T. had elected a pro-slavery government.

Border Ruffians invading K.T.

The Free-State settlers set up a government of their own. For a time, there were two

governments in K.T. Both governments created armies or militias. These militias fought for control of K.T. The fighting was fierce. K.T. became known as "Bleeding Kansas."

The town of Lawrence, Kansas, was settled by people who believed that slavery was wrong. Some hid runaway slaves in their homes. The Underground Railroad had many "stations" in Lawrence. They helped runaway slaves escape north to freedom.

In September 1856, 2,500 armed pro-slavery soldiers and Ruffians surrounded Lawrence. There were only 300 men in the Free-State Militia. The town was in terrible danger. But just before it was attacked, the governor sent U.S. troops to save Lawrence.

The war in K.T. took place five years before the Civil War began. The Civil War is sometimes called the War Between the States. The war in K.T. could be called the same thing.

The destruction of Lawrence and the Free State Hotel.

In 1857, there was a U.S. presidential election. Franklin Pierce was not reelected. He was not even nominated by his own party to run for president.

Kansas became a state in 1861. It did not allow slavery.

About the Author

Kate McMullan says, "In the fifth grade, my friends and I discovered what we called the "orange books." They were biographies, with bright orange covers, of important people in American history: Sacagawea, Ben Franklin, Molly Pitcher, and many more. We all read them. At recess we talked about Dolley Madison's dinner parties and whether Pocahontas truly loved John Smith. The "orange books" brought history alive for us.

"I loved reading the letters and diaries of the pioneers who settled in K.T. Here were stories of real people — everyday people — like us. These pioneers included so many strange

and unexpected details in the writing. A bed cord really was used to raise the flag on Blue Mound. Old Sacramento, the Free-State Militia cannon, really was stolen by the Ruffians and dressed in women's clothing to hide it. My aim in writing this diary was to see if I could put nine-year-old Meg Wells into some of these pioneer stories in hopes of bringing history to life for today's readers."

Kate McMullan is the author of *The Story of Harriet Tubman, Conductor on the Underground Railroad*, and *I STINK!*, a *Boston Globe*–Horn Book Honor recipient. She also writes the Greek myth–inspired Myth-o-Mania series. Kate lives with her daughter and her husband, the noted illustrator, James McMullan, in New York City and Sag Harbor.

Acknowledgments

The author would like to thank her editors, Beth S. Levine, for her thoughtful comments, Lisa Sandell for finding the right title, and Jean Marzollo, for her biblical scholarship. She would especially like to thank Judith M. Sweets of the Watkins Community Museum of History for her wonderful research, her great sensitivity to the requirements of this project, and for introducing the author to the works of Kansas Territory pioneers Louisa Prentiss Simpson, author of "Grandmother's Letters," and Anna Smith Irvin, author of "Memories of Early Days in Kansas."

Grateful acknowledgment is made for permission to reprint the following:

Cover portrait by Glen Harrington.
Page 101: Ferrying voters, North Wind Picture Archives.
Page 102: Border Ruffians invading, North Wind Picture Archives.
Page 104: Destruction of the Free State Hotel, the Kansas State Historical Society.

Other books in the My America series

Corey's Underground Railroad Diaries
by Sharon Dennis Wyeth

Elizabeth's Jamestown Colony Diaries
by Patricia Hermes

Hope's Revolutionary War Diaries
by Kristianna Gregory

Joshua's Oregon Trail Diaries
by Patricia Hermes

Meg's Prairie Diaries
by Kate McMullan

Virginia's Civil War Diaries
by Mary Pope Osborne

For Cora Williams, with much love

While the events described and some of the characters in this book may be based on actual historical events and real people, Margaret Cora Wells is a fictional character, created by the author, and her diary is a work of fiction.

Library of Congress Cataloging-in-Publication Data
McMullan, Kate.
For This Land / by Kate McMullan
p.   cm. — (My America. McMullan, Kate. Meg's diary; bk. 2)
Summary: Meg records in her diary the events from July to November of 1856, when her
family is reunited and must face challenges from fires to pro-slavery border ruffians who
are trying to take over Kansas Territory.
ISBN 0-439-37059-0; 0-439-37060-4 (pbk.)
[1. Frontier and pioneer life — Kansas — Fiction. 2. Diaries — Fiction. 3. Kansas —
History — 1854–1861 — Fiction.] I. Title. II. Series
PZ7.M2295 En 2003

[Fic] — 21   2002026942
CIP AC

10 9 8 7 6 5 4 3 2   03 04 05 06 07

The display type was set in Rogers.
The text type was set in Goudy.
Photo research by Amla Sanghvi.
Book design by Elizabeth B. Parisi.

Printed in the U.S.A.   23
First edition, May 2003